P9-DDW-078

Disney · PIXAR

TOY STORY 4

THE OFFICIAL GUIDE

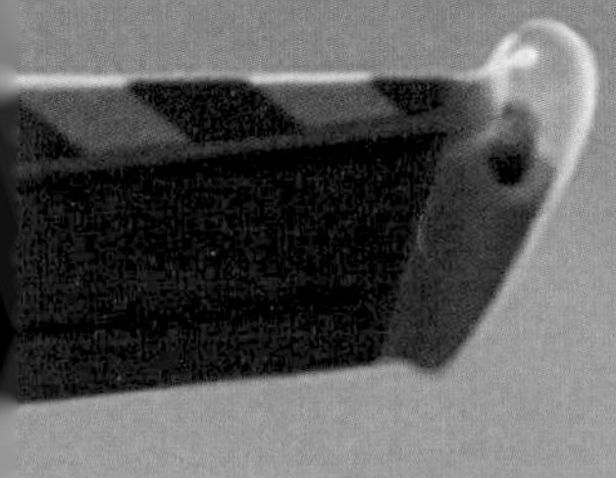

THE OFFICIAL GUIDE

Written by Ruth Amos

Contents

Introduction

The toys are back in town! Woody, Buzz, and the gang are getting used to life with their new owner, Bonnie. But adventure lies just around the corner as the gang sets off on a road trip and a clueless new toy causes chaos! Will everybody make it back in one piece?

Woody

Faithful friend

Cowboy doll Woody is the most loyal toy that any kid could wish for. This kind, lovable sheriff and his gang of toy friends are getting used to life with their new owner, Bonnie.

Things you need to know about Woody

1. Woody is a vintage toy, made in the late 1950s.
2. He has a voice box sewn inside him with a pull cord.
3. Sometimes he cares a bit too much about his kid owner and doesn't realize there is more to life.
4. Woody's old owner, Andy, gifted all his toys to Bonnie when he grew up.

Facing the future

Life isn't always easy for Woody in Bonnie's room. She already has her own set of toys, and Woody is a new toy on the block. Sometimes he misses the old days with Andy.

Blast from the past

Woody is shocked to spot a bedside lamp in a store window. His old friend Bo Peep was part of the lamp, which once belonged to Andy's sister, Molly. Woody hasn't seen Bo since Molly gave her and the lamp away, years ago.

Hat can be
thrown like
a boomerang
at targets
Did you
know?
Woody can use
his pull string like
a lasso to
catch people!
Cowboy
riding boots
with golden
spurs

Hardworking cowboy

When Bonnie's new toy needs rescuing, Woody considers it his duty to bring him back to Bonnie—whatever the cost. Once Woody has made his mind up, he can be a bit stubborn!

Who's who?

Meet the gang! Lots of different toys live in Bonnie's bedroom. Plush and plastic, alien and animal—toys of all shapes and sizes can be found here!

Woody

Jessie

Bullseye

Hamm

Mr. Pricklepants

Slinky Dog

Trixie

Rex

Buzz
Buttercup
Dolly

Alien
Mrs. Potato Head
Mr. Potato Head
Forky

Bonnie

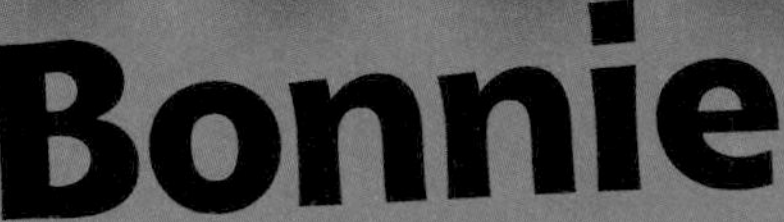

Creative kid

Five-year-old Bonnie is a bright, kind child with a big imagination! She loves to play with her toys, invent new games, and go on make-believe adventures.

Things you need to know about Bonnie

1. She likes to build a makeshift town and play with her toys in it.
2. Bonnie goes on a road trip with her family, and she's very excited.
3. She is really sad when she loses her new toy, Forky.
4. Bonnie loves to play on the swing with her toys.

Growing up

Bonnie has to start kindergarten, and she is not very happy about it. She would much rather be playing a game with her toys at home!

Stowaway sheriff

Bonnie wants to take a toy with her to kindergarten on her first day, but she's not allowed to. Bonnie doesn't know that Woody sneaks into her backpack to keep an eye on her!

Purple backpack often gets left behind by Bonnie
Did you know?
Bonnie loves drawing, coloring, and making things.
Stripy leggings are great for running and climbing

Old-time toys

Kindhearted Bonnie looks after all her toys well. Some of the older toys from her toddler days get left in the closet nowadays, but they understand it's all just part of her growing up.

SCHOOL
Children chat to
each other in
excitement

Kindergarten

Kindergarten seems like a fun place. There are lots of activities to do, interesting things to learn, and new friends to meet—but poor Bonnie is finding it all a bit scary!

Bright pictures and a map cover the walls
Bonnie looks around the room shyly

Woody to the rescue

It's craft time at kindergarten, but Bonnie is upset when another kid takes away her art supplies. Luckily, Woody has a plan!

1

Scan the room—the art supplies are being thrown into a trash can.

2

Check that the coast is clear before you leave your hiding spot.

3

Carefully climb down from the cubbies to the floor.

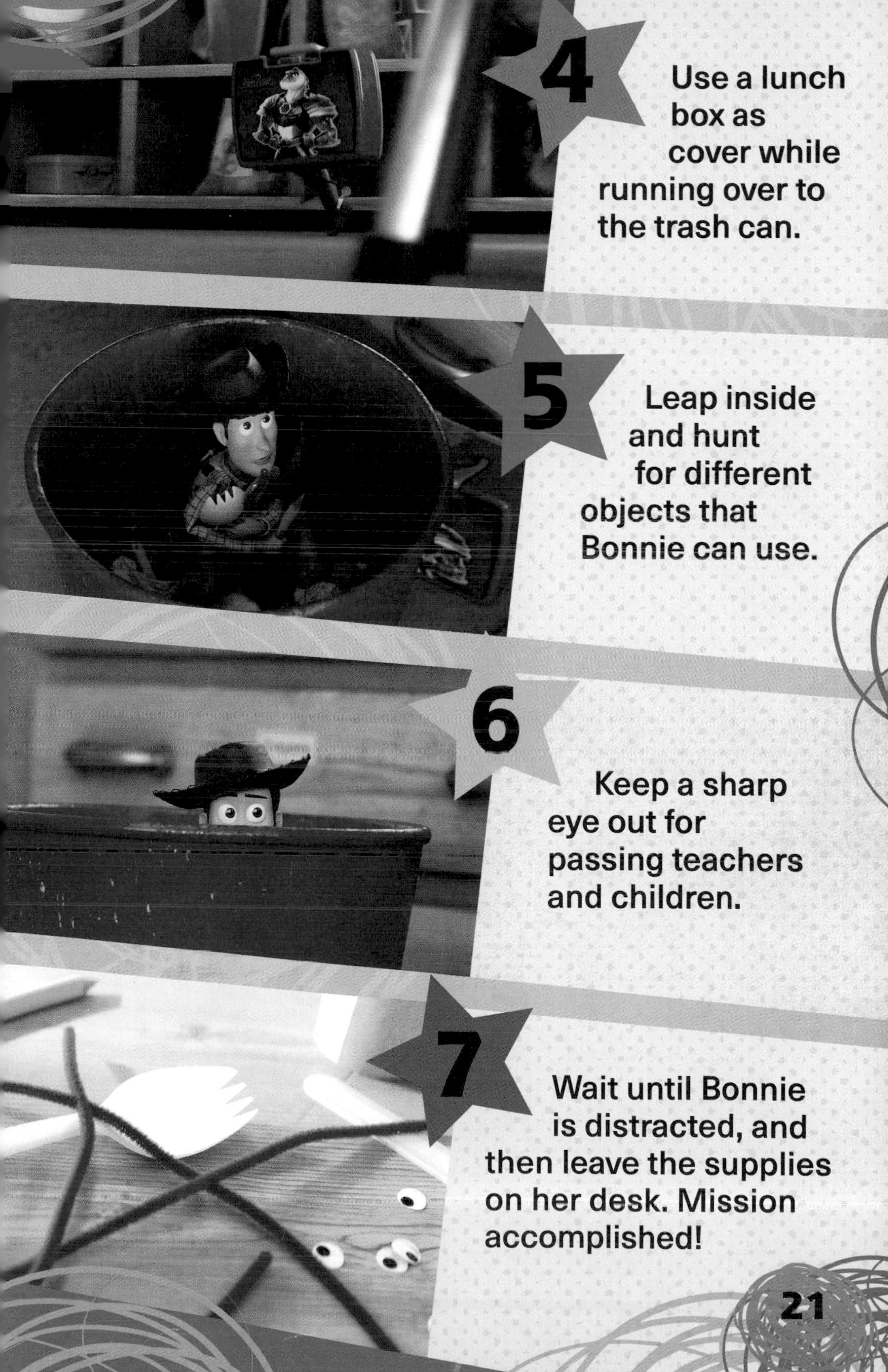

4

Use a lunch box as cover while running over to the trash can.

5

Leap inside and hunt for different objects that Bonnie can use.

6

Keep a sharp eye out for passing teachers and children.

7

Wait until Bonnie is distracted, and then leave the supplies on her desk. Mission accomplished!

Making Forky

Bonnie puts her brilliant imagination to the test. She uses the random objects that Woody found in the trash can to build something new—a brand-new friend named Forky!

Red pipe cleaner for arms

A spork for the body and face

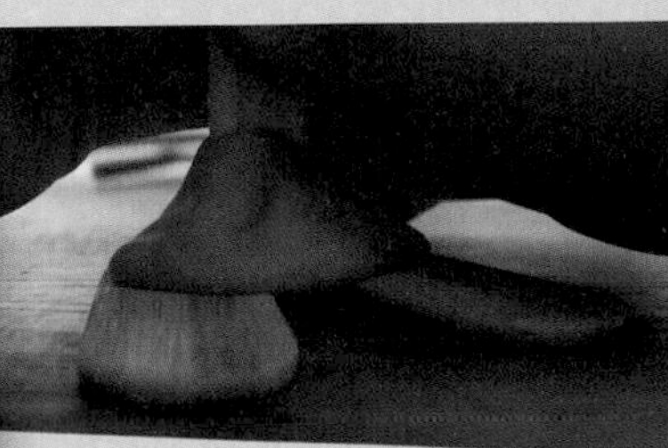

Sticky putty glues body to feet

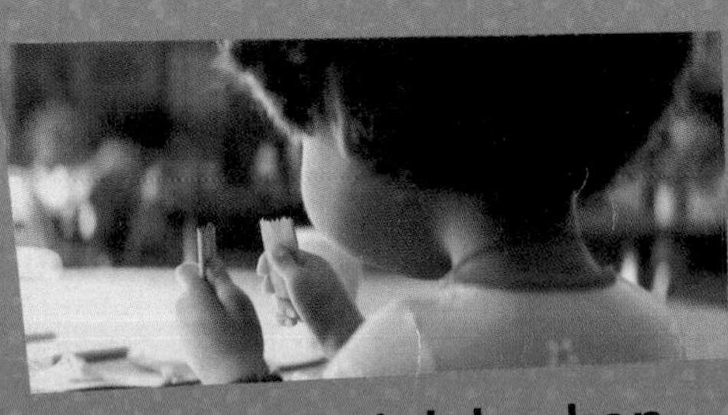

Ice pop stick broken in half for feet

Googly eyes
Feet marked with Bonnie's name in felt-tip pen

Forky

Confused new toy

After Bonnie makes Forky, he is like a baby—he has to learn how to walk and talk. But all this scared spork wants is to climb into the nearest trash can, where he feels warm, cozy, and safe.

Things you need to know about Forky

1. Forky is scared of Bonnie at first because she's so much bigger.
2. As a spork, Forky says he was made for eating soup, salad, and chili.
3. Woody has to babysit Forky constantly since he keeps trying to climb into the trash.
4. Later, he wants to be with Bonnie, because he believes he is her trash!

Bonnie's room

Bright and cozy, Bonnie's colorful room is full of fun, just like its owner. The squishy bed is perfect for jumping on. Baskets and boxes are filled with toys and games, ready for playtime!

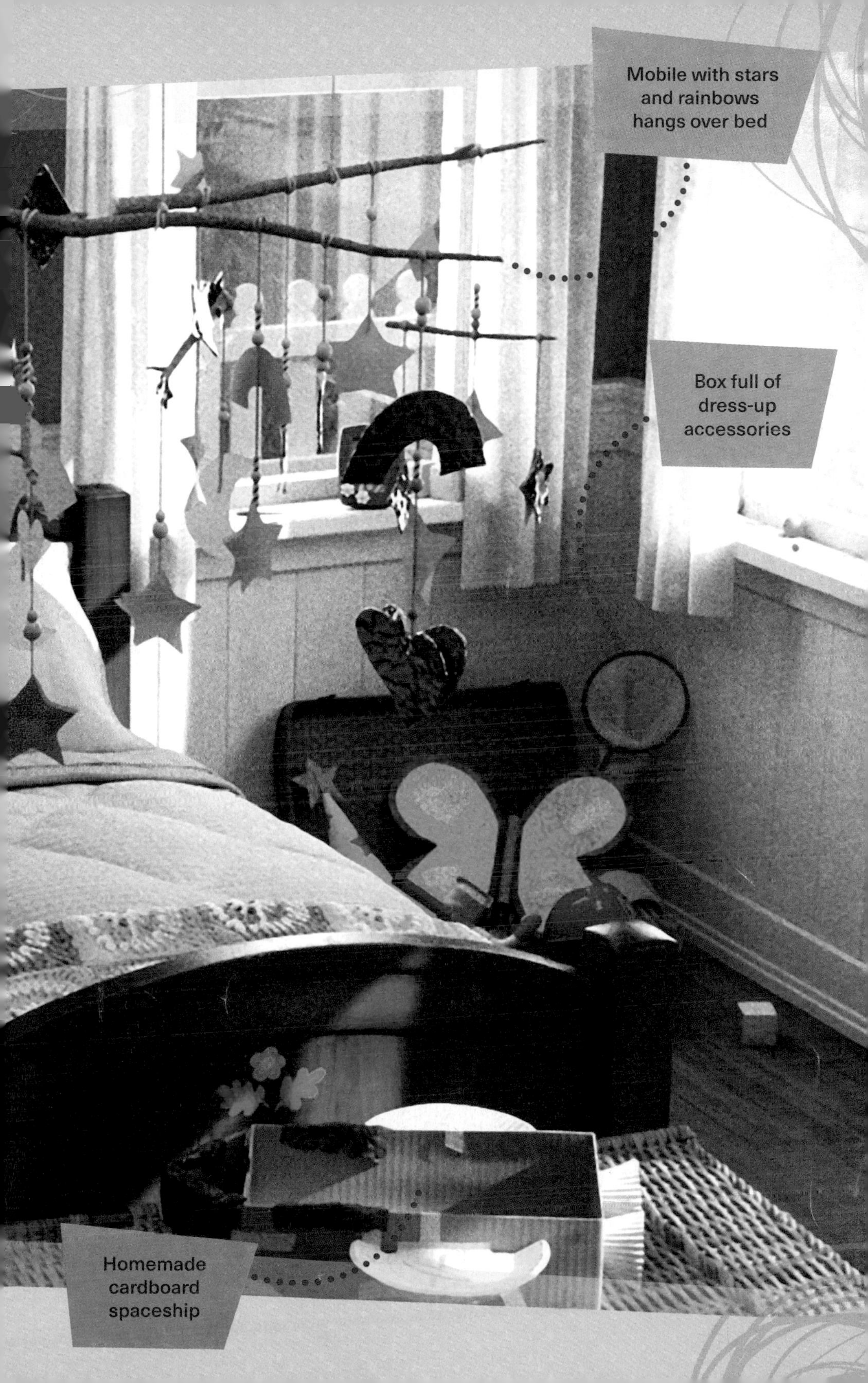
Mobile with stars
and rainbows
hangs over bed
Box full of
dress-up
accessories
Homemade
cardboard
spaceship

Buzz Lightyear

Brave space ranger

Awesome space explorer Buzz is always ready for a new challenge. Buzzing with energy, he loves to team up with sidekick Woody. To infinity and beyond!

Things you need to know about Buzz Lightyear

1. Buzz is Woody's best friend.
2. When Woody doesn't return from a mission to bring back Forky, Buzz sets off to find him.
3. Buzz thinks the voice that plays when he presses his space suit buttons must belong to his conscience!
4. He gets pinned up as a prize at a fairground by accident.

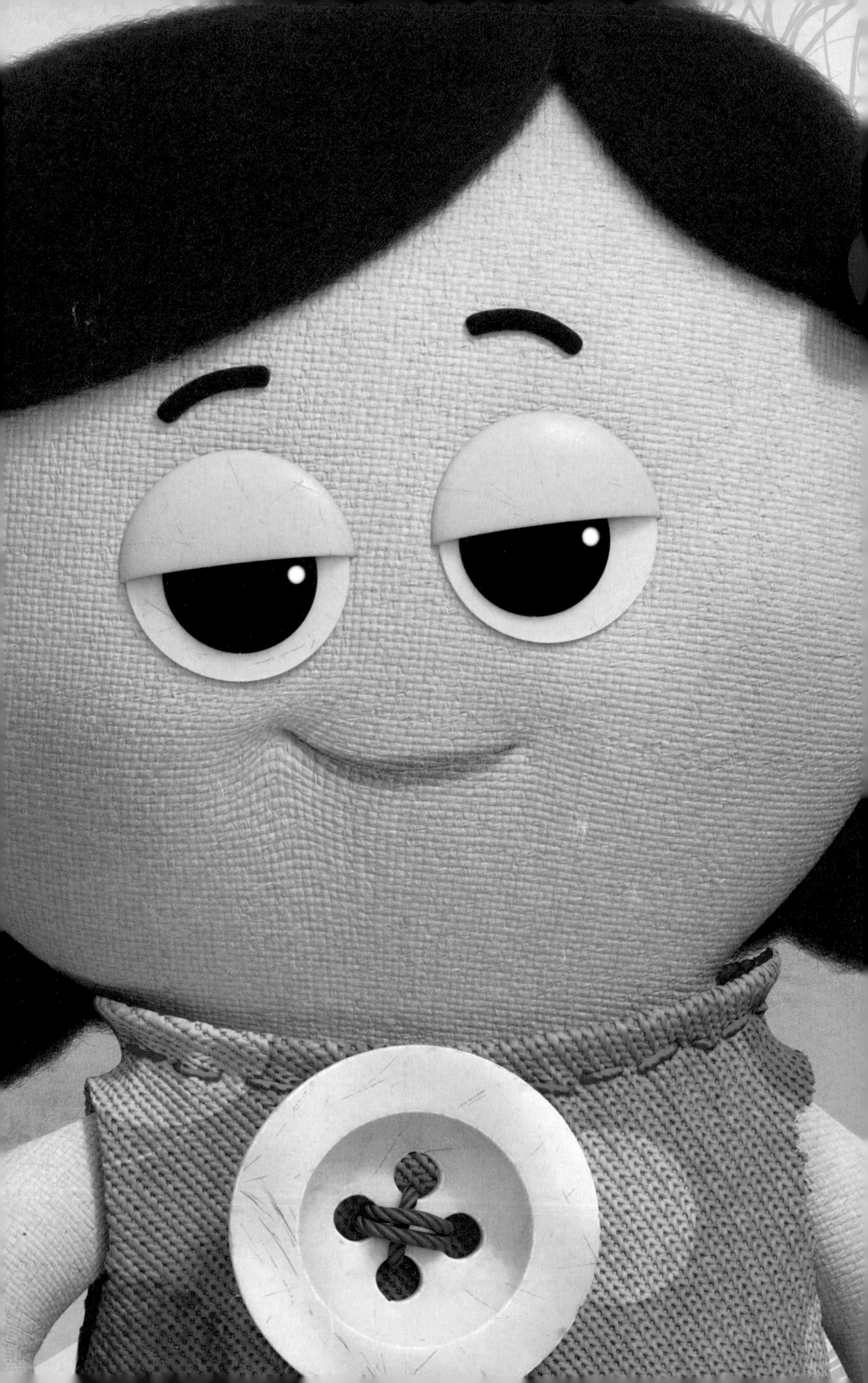

Dolly

Born leader

Rag doll Dolly takes charge of the toys in Bonnie's room and makes sure everything runs smoothly. She is great at keeping calm in a crisis!

Things you need to know about Dolly

1. Dolly plays the part of the mayor in Bonnie's pretend town game.
2. She welcomes any new toys and makes sure they are happy.
3. Dolly warns all the toys whenever Bonnie is about to enter a room so they can freeze in toy mode.
4. She thinks Woody can be a little bit dramatic sometimes.

Bonnie's parents

Caring mom and dad

Bonnie's parents are really proud of their little girl. They know she is scared to start kindergarten, but they are sure that she will have fun there.

Things you need to know about Bonnie's parents

1. They try to reassure Bonnie that kindergarten will be fine.
2. As a reward for being brave, they surprise Bonnie with a road trip vacation!
3. They spend a long time hunting for Bonnie's missing new toy, Forky.
4. They cheer her up when she's upset.

Road trip

Adventure time! Bonnie and her parents set off on vacation in their RV. There is plenty of space inside for Forky, Woody, and the rest of the toy gang.

Comfy ride

The big RV has comfy beds for tired travelers. It also has a slide-out awning so the family can relax in the shade.

Artist at work

The dining table is a good spot for Bonnie to draw. Her toys are lined up alongside, ready for playtime.

Did you know?

The family makes a stop at the old-fashioned town of Grand Basin.

Great escapes?

Forky keeps trying to escape from Bonnie and leap into the nearest trash can. Exhausted Woody always brings him back, but this confused utensil just tries again!

Hiding on the flower on Bonnie's backpack when she goes outside

Launching himself toward the trash can on the RV

Jumping out of the window of the RV

How to be a good toy

Forky knows nothing about being a toy—he doesn't even understand what a toy is! It's up to patient Woody to explain the rules.

Always be there for Bonnie and look out for her when she is scared or sad.

Stay in **toy mode** whenever Bonnie or her family are in the room.

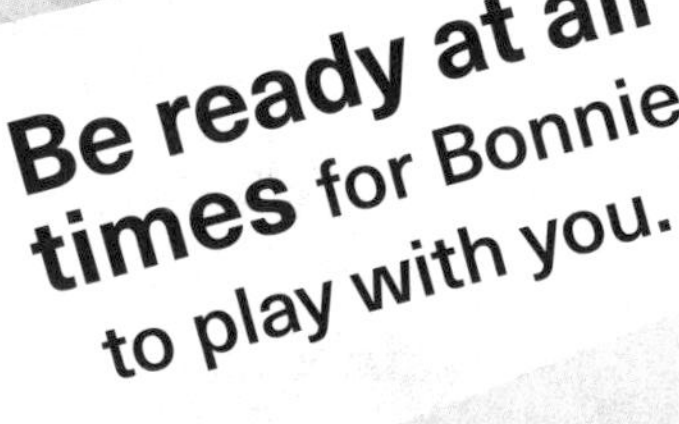

Be ready at all times for Bonnie to play with you.

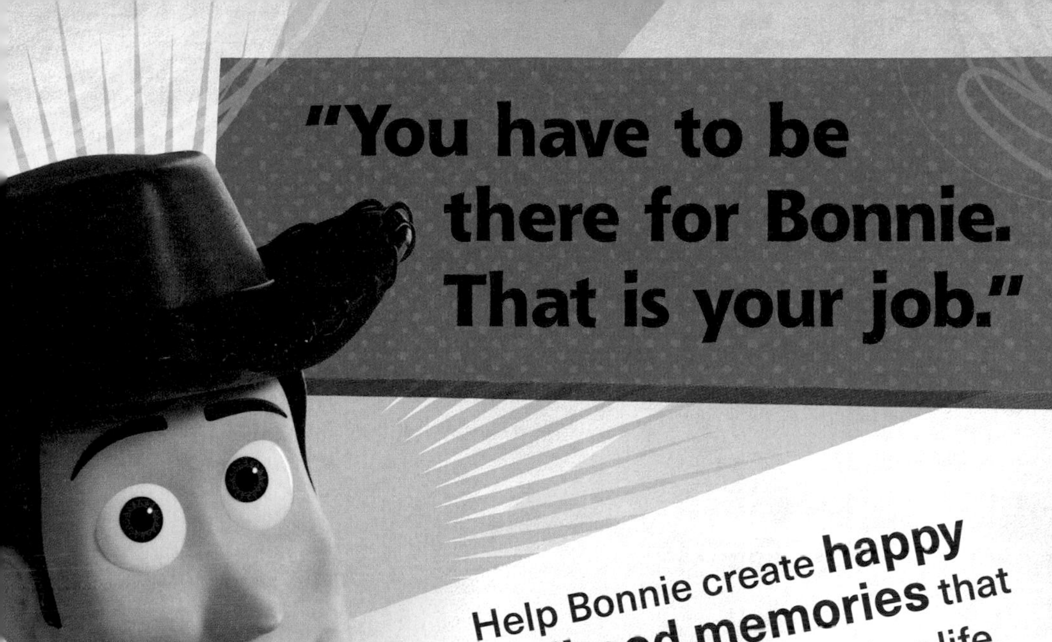

"You have to be there for Bonnie. That is your job."

Help Bonnie create **happy childhood memories** that she will remember all her life.

Watch over Bonnie as she grows up and becomes an adult.

If you get lost, you should **make your way back to Bonnie** as soon as possible!

Combat Carl Jr. action figures lie in the sandbox
Kids play games with lost toys they've found

The playground

Watch out! The playground is always full of children, ready to play with any toys they might find here. For lost toys like Bo Peep, it's super exciting when a new group of kids arrive here—but Woody would much prefer to be with his owner!

Woody is launched
on baby swing
high into air
Bonnie's name
written on sole
of Woody's boot

Bo Peep

Confident adventurer

Shepherdess Bo Peep has spent years as a lost toy with no owner. She travels between playgrounds, plays with different children, and then moves on. Bo loves the freedom and excitement that it brings her!

Things you need to know about Bo Peep

1. Andy's family gave Bo away. She was later sold to an antiques store, which she decided to leave.
2. She is made of porcelain, a fragile ceramic material.
3. Bo often gets chipped or broken by kids, but she doesn't mind. She just glues herself back together!
4. She bumps into Woody in the playground. Surprise!

A lost toy

Long, hooked staff is light but strong

Woody is horrified to discover that Bo is now a lost toy, with no owner. But Bo wouldn't swap her life for anything! She is independent, and she is following her dreams.

Star support

Woody is in awe of Bo's ability to champion other toys and make them believe in themselves. It will be crucial for their upcoming mission!

Tactical expert

Bo agrees to help Woody rescue Forky from the antiques store. She is great at planning risky missions, and she knows the place well. Bo also has some special toy contacts who might be able to help!

Did you know?

Bo has been a lost toy for seven years. She has seen so many fantastic things during that time!

Cool moves

Bo Peep is on the move! She can leap, climb, and sprint, but it's not just her feet that are fast—her expert handiwork turns her staff into a multipurpose tool.

Speedy Bo is great at dodging kids' trampling feet and weaving in and out of obstacles.

Bo isn't afraid of heights and always lands on her feet after a big fall.

The staff makes a good weapon for whacking enemies or tripping them up.

Bo can hold out her staff to pull a climbing toy up to a high spot.

Bo can even use her hook to slide down a zipline or clear away cobwebs!

Bo uses her long staff in a rescue operation to help reach a toy in danger.

Operation Pull-Toy

Years ago, Woody and Bo Peep once pulled off an amazing rescue mission! The pair worked together with Andy's other toys to save RC the car. Talk about teamwork!

1

Locate the victim

Spotted! RC is stranded outside the house in a raging storm!

2

Create a launchpad

Bo builds a launchpad with a book and an armadillo toy. Jessie gets on it.

3

Open the window

Jessie is launched up to the sill and opens the window.

4

Lower Woody down

Woody climbs on Slinky Dog and rappels down the side of the house as the others hold Slinky's feet.

5

Disaster!

Slinky has run out of stretch! Woody can't reach RC.

6

Plan B

Bo attaches a long line of toy monkeys to her hook and adds it to Slinky's spring.

7

Heave!

Woody lunges forward and grabs RC. The toys pull them back up to the window. RC is safe!

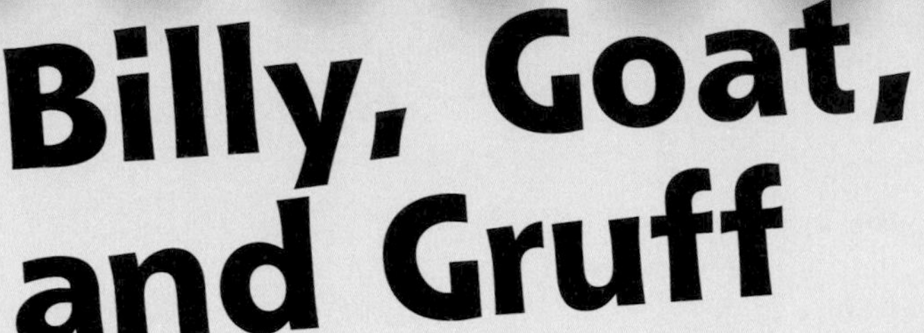

Billy, Goat, and Gruff

Bo Peep's faithful flock

This trio of porcelain sheep love their fun lives as lost toys. Attached together in one big fleece, they follow Bo loyally wherever her adventures take them.

Things you need to know about Billy, Goat, and Gruff

1. The sheep help Bo collect random objects to use for repairs in case they get damaged.
2. They used to be part of Molly's bedside lamp, along with Bo.
3. They love winning races.
4. They're not impressed when Woody forgets their names and thinks they are boys.

Giggle McDimples

Tiny detective

Officer Giggle McDimples runs the Pet Patrol, searching the streets for missing pets. Smart and funny, Giggle is Bo's best friend and travel buddy.

Things you need to know about Giggle McDimples

1. Giggle is half an inch tall.
2. She searches for pets such as ants, caterpillars, and miniature poodles.
3. Giggle sits on Bo's shoulder to speak to her.
4. She can fit inside the keyhole of a door, spin around like a picklock, and unlock it!

Wall map shows last sightings of missing pets
Pet Patrol deputy joins Giggle in her office for meeting
Patrol car parked outside on drive

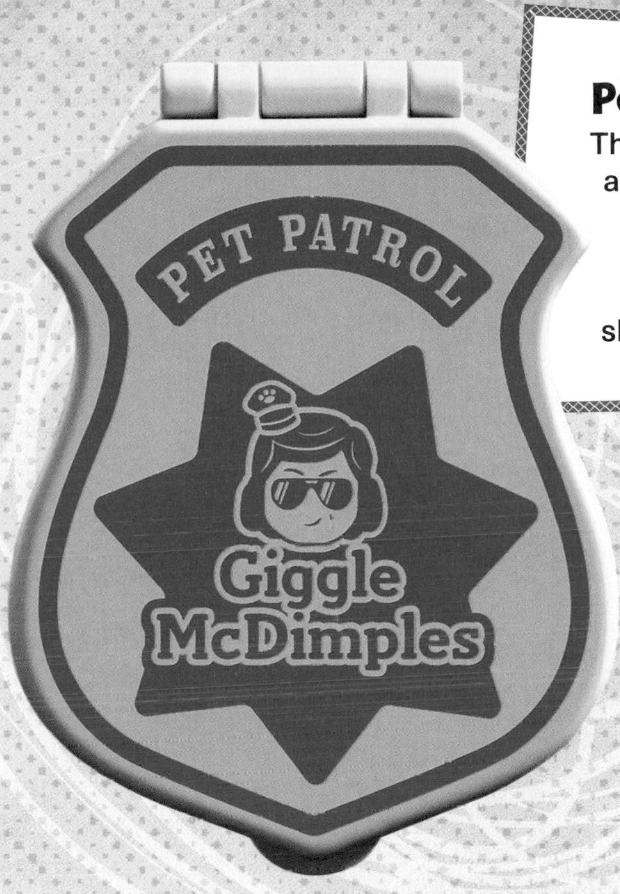

Perfectly portable

The Pet Patrol is shaped like a police officer's badge. When Giggle and Bo are traveling to a new place, it fits neatly inside Bo's skunkmobile vehicle.

Pet Patrol headquarters

When she isn't patroling Mini-opolis city for missing animals, Giggle works at the Pet Patrol headquarters. This tiny office has everything she needs to organize her next search and rescue mission.

Tail is
made from
feather duster
Furry material
hides the
car's wheels

Roomy ride

There's plenty of space inside the vehicle for Bo, the three sheep, Giggle, and Woody during their adventures!

Skunkmobile

Bo Peep built this skunklike vehicle using a motorized toy car and objects found on her travels. It's a good way to get around quickly—most people leap out of the way when they see a scary skunk on the prowl!

Did you know?

Billy, Goat, and Gruff drive the vehicle. They aren't great drivers—they nearly run over poor Woody by accident.

Nose is made from old bottle cap

Combat Carl Jrs.

Nonstop action figures

The cool Combat Carl Jr. soldiers are based in the playground. These lost toys don't just wait around for children to find them—they always keep a lookout for the next good playtime opportunity!

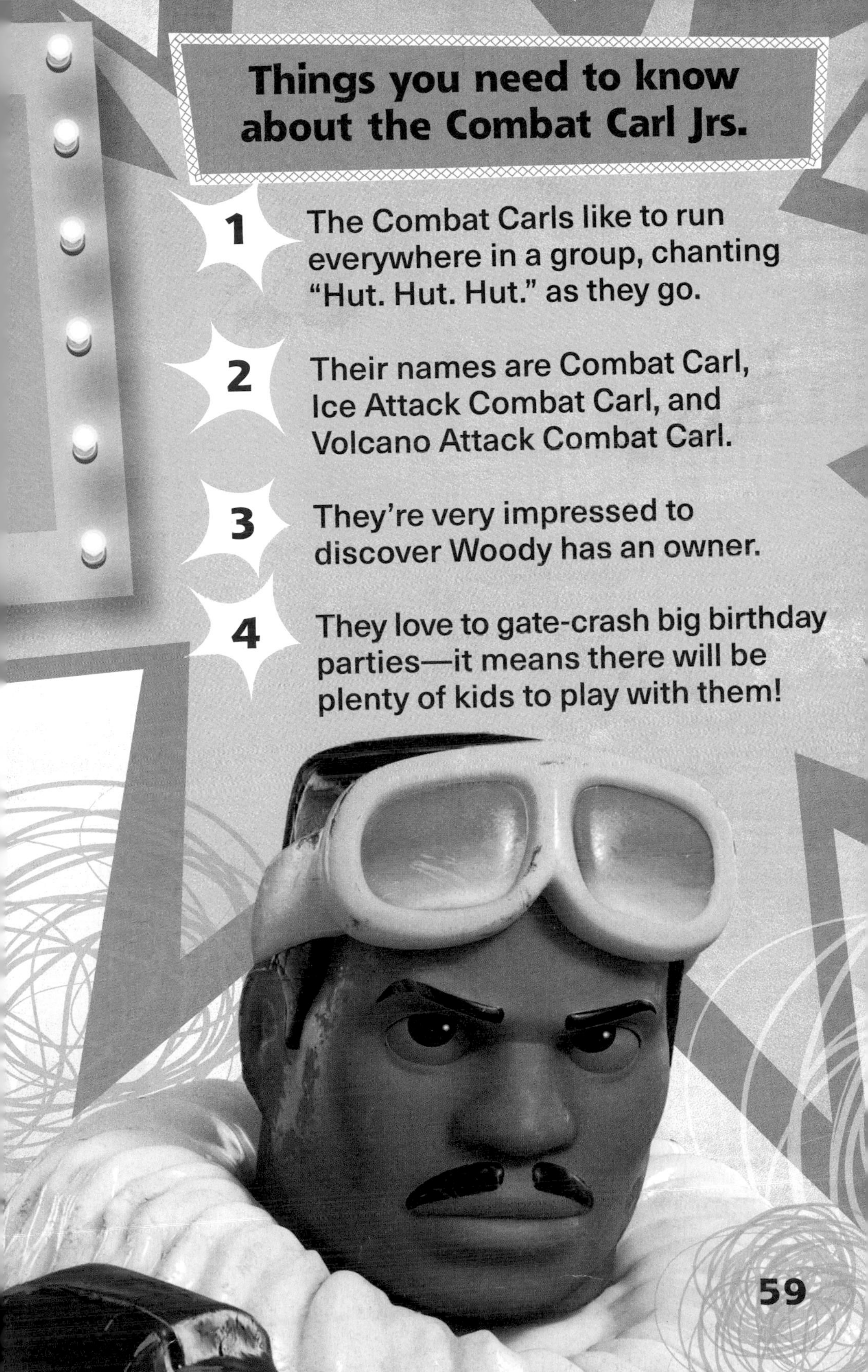

Things you need to know about the Combat Carl Jrs.

1 The Combat Carls like to run everywhere in a group, chanting "Hut. Hut. Hut." as they go.

2 Their names are Combat Carl, Ice Attack Combat Carl, and Volcano Attack Combat Carl.

3 They're very impressed to discover Woody has an owner.

4 They love to gate-crash big birthday parties—it means there will be plenty of kids to play with them!

Who is your perfect sidekick?

Adventures can be a risky business, so you need the perfect toy partner by your side. Who would be your accomplice?

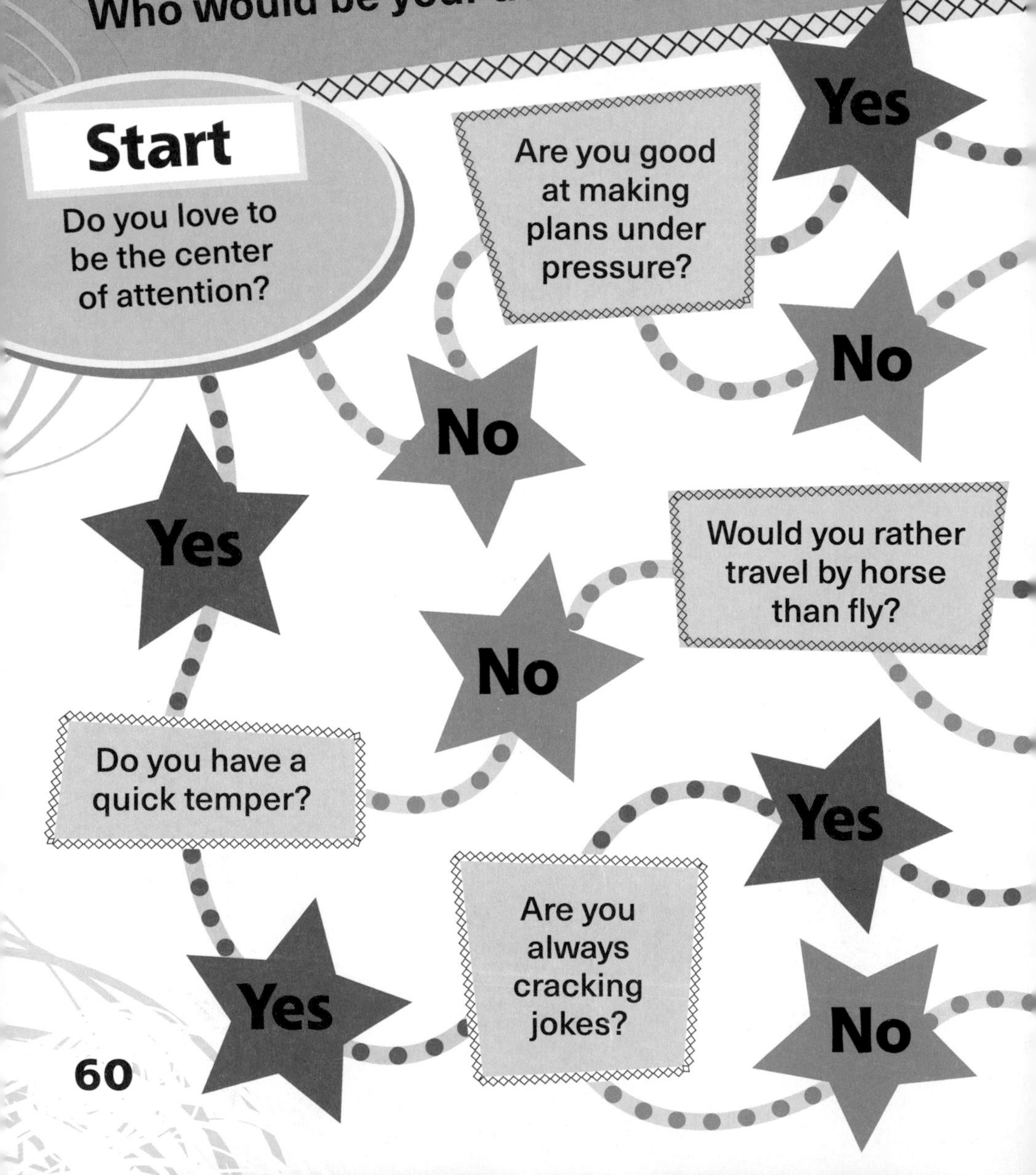

Start

Do you love to be the center of attention?

Yes

No

Are you good at making plans under pressure?

Yes

No

Would you rather travel by horse than fly?

No

Yes

No

Do you have a quick temper?

Yes

Are you always cracking jokes?

Is money important to you?

Hamm

No

Giggle McDimples

Are you great at acting?

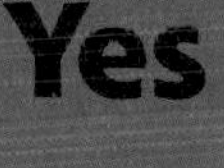

Trixie

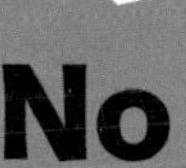

Rex

Yes

Jessie

No

Buzz Lightyear

Mr. Potato Head

Mr. Pricklepants

Antiques store

From old furniture and signs to unusual trinkets and treasures, the Second Chance Antiques store is full of surprises. Customers never know what they might find here!

Teatime

The store owner's granddaughter, Harmony, uses an old china set and a little stool for pretend tea parties.

Margaret, the store owner, chats to her daughter, Carol

Cabinet filled with valuable jewelry and knickknacks

Gabby Gabby

Lonely doll

Vintage doll Gabby Gabby lives in a cabinet in the antiques store. She spends the long days dreaming of a happy future with a child owner who loves her. If only she weren't broken!

Things you need to know about Gabby Gabby

1. Since her voice box is broken, kids don't play with her.
2. Gabby Gabby loves tea parties and practices holding her cup correctly.
3. Her antique stroller is her preferred mode of transportation.
4. She has a gang of dummies in the store who do everything she says.

Bright future?

Gabby Gabby is delighted when she meets Woody and Forky in the store. She notices Woody's voice box right away and wants to learn all about him. Perhaps he can help her?

Stop that fork!

Gabby Gabby orders her dummies to capture Forky and Woody when they get scared and try to leave. They manage to catch Forky, but Woody escapes!

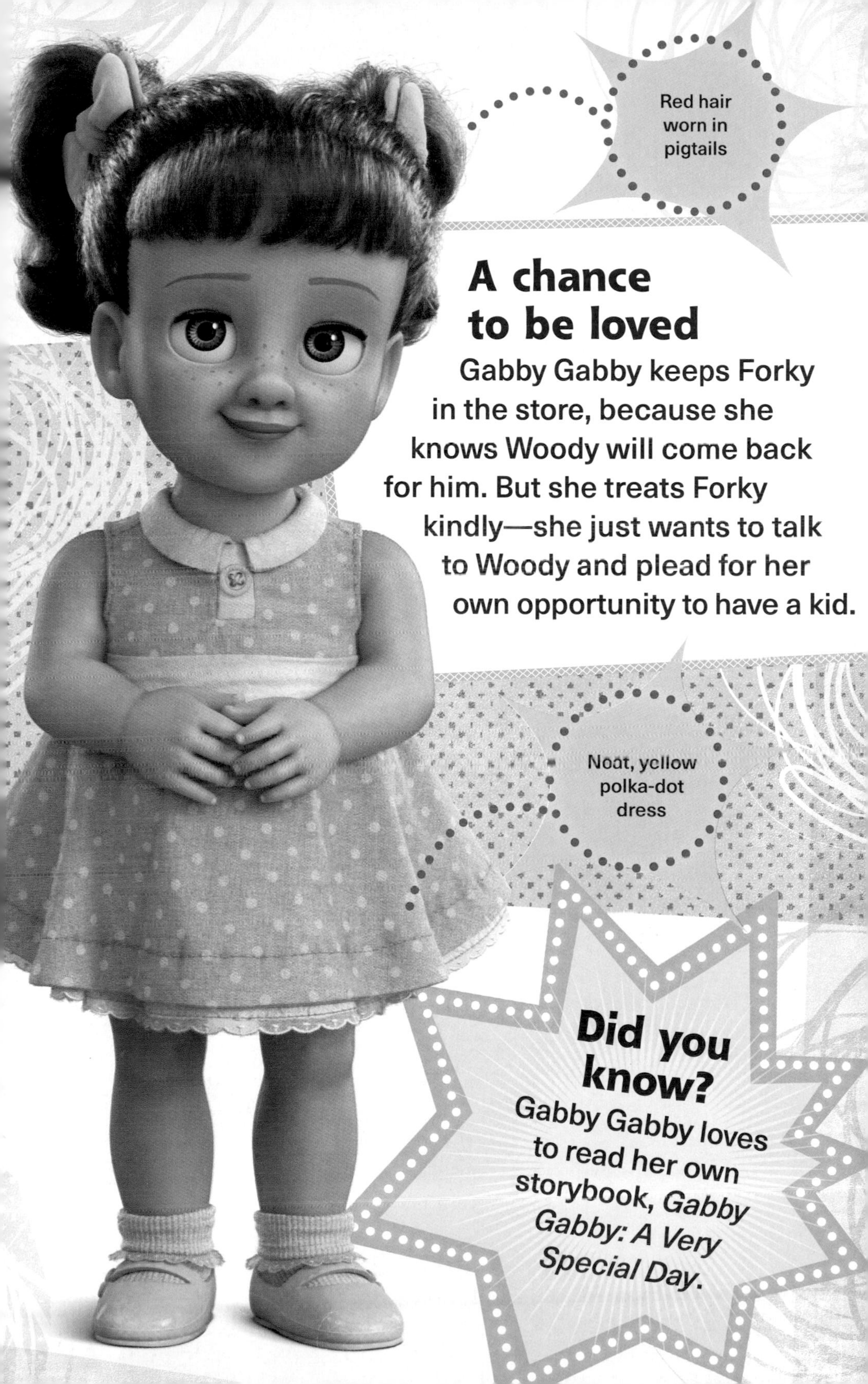

A chance to be loved

Gabby Gabby keeps Forky in the store, because she knows Woody will come back for him. But she treats Forky kindly—she just wants to talk to Woody and plead for her own opportunity to have a kid.

Did you know?

Gabby Gabby loves to read her own storybook, *Gabby Gabby: A Very Special Day.*

Benson

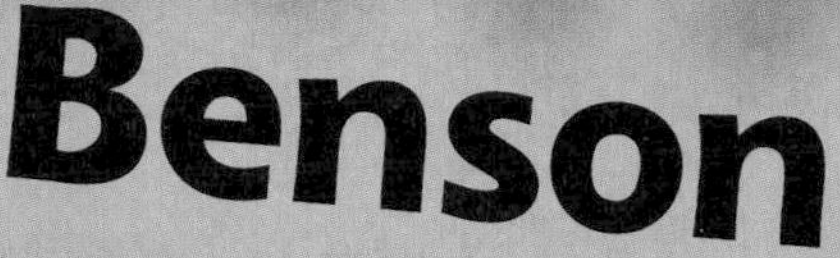

Creepy henchman

Ventriloquist's dummy Benson is Gabby Gabby's chief sidekick. This smartly dressed menace leads a gang of dummies and is always on the lookout for trouble.

Things you need to know about Benson

1. He guards Gabby Gabby's cabinet and pushes her around in her stroller.
2. He wears a pinstripe suit and a red bow tie.
3. Benson captures Forky under Gabby Gabby's orders.
4. There are three scary dummies in Benson's team.

Giant Ferris wheel has amazing views
BARBER
TACO CHOCO
MUNCHIE
Airplanes dip and spin around on ride

The carnival

The traveling carnival has come to Grand Basin! This fun-filled fairground is bursting with scary rides, whirling carousels, and exciting game booths.

Brightly colored game and food stalls

Customers wait in line to go on ride

"If you think you can just show up and take our top prize spot, you're wrong."
Bunny

Ducky and Bunny

Bickering buddies

Plush toys Ducky and Bunny have spent years as fairground prizes, waiting to be won by a child. This scrappy pair has a lot of arguments!

Things you need to know about Ducky and Bunny

1. Ducky and Bunny are attached together by the hand.
2. They have been prizes at the Star Adventurer booth for three years.
3. When Buzz arrives as a prize, they think he's trying to cheat and be won by a kid first!
4. They end up joining Buzz on the mission to find Forky.

Big squabbles!

Bunny and Ducky always seem to be arguing about something. Perhaps it's because this plush pair have to spend so much time together—all day, every day!

What do you mean? Bunny gets mad when Ducky doesn't explain things properly. After all, Bunny isn't a mind reader!

Help! Ducky can't believe he actually has to point out how short his legs are to get Bunny's help to kick Buzz!

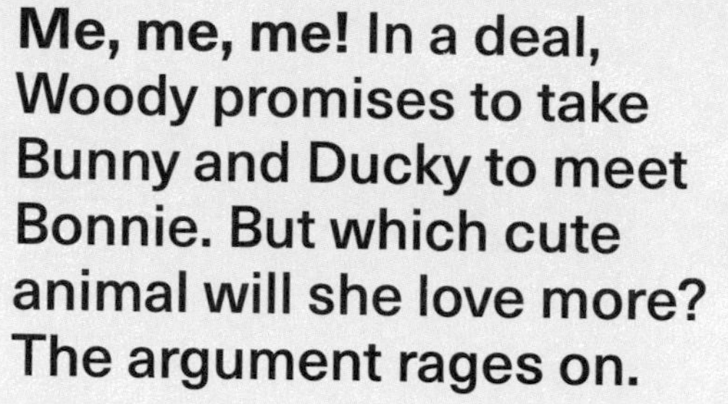

Me, me, me! In a deal, Woody promises to take Bunny and Ducky to meet Bonnie. But which cute animal will she love more? The argument rages on.

Hurry up! When Buzz escapes the booth, the pair chase after him. Ducky is irritated when Bunny gets stuck—giving Buzz a big head start!

Pardon? Ducky says Bunny needs to work on paying attention and his listening skills.

Duke Caboom

Cool stunt toy

Famous Canadian motorcycle star Duke Caboom may be a show-off, but he doesn't really believe in himself. After he was rejected by his kid owner, poor Duke lost all his confidence.

Things you need to know about Duke Caboom

1. Duke hangs out with other toys inside the pinball machine at the antiques store.

2. Duke's kid, Rejean, threw Duke away when he couldn't land a big motorcycle jump and crashed.

3. He has a handlebar mustache and wears a maple leaf–patterned cape.

4. Duke tries to help Bo, Woody, and their team rescue Forky.

Stunt motorcycle

Duke Caboom is never seen without his vintage motorcycle. It might be a bit battered these days, but it can still take him on an epic ride!

Duke rides down the antiques store aisle, making Dragon the store cat chase after him. This distracts Dragon away from the other toys!

Tire worn from Duke's crashes

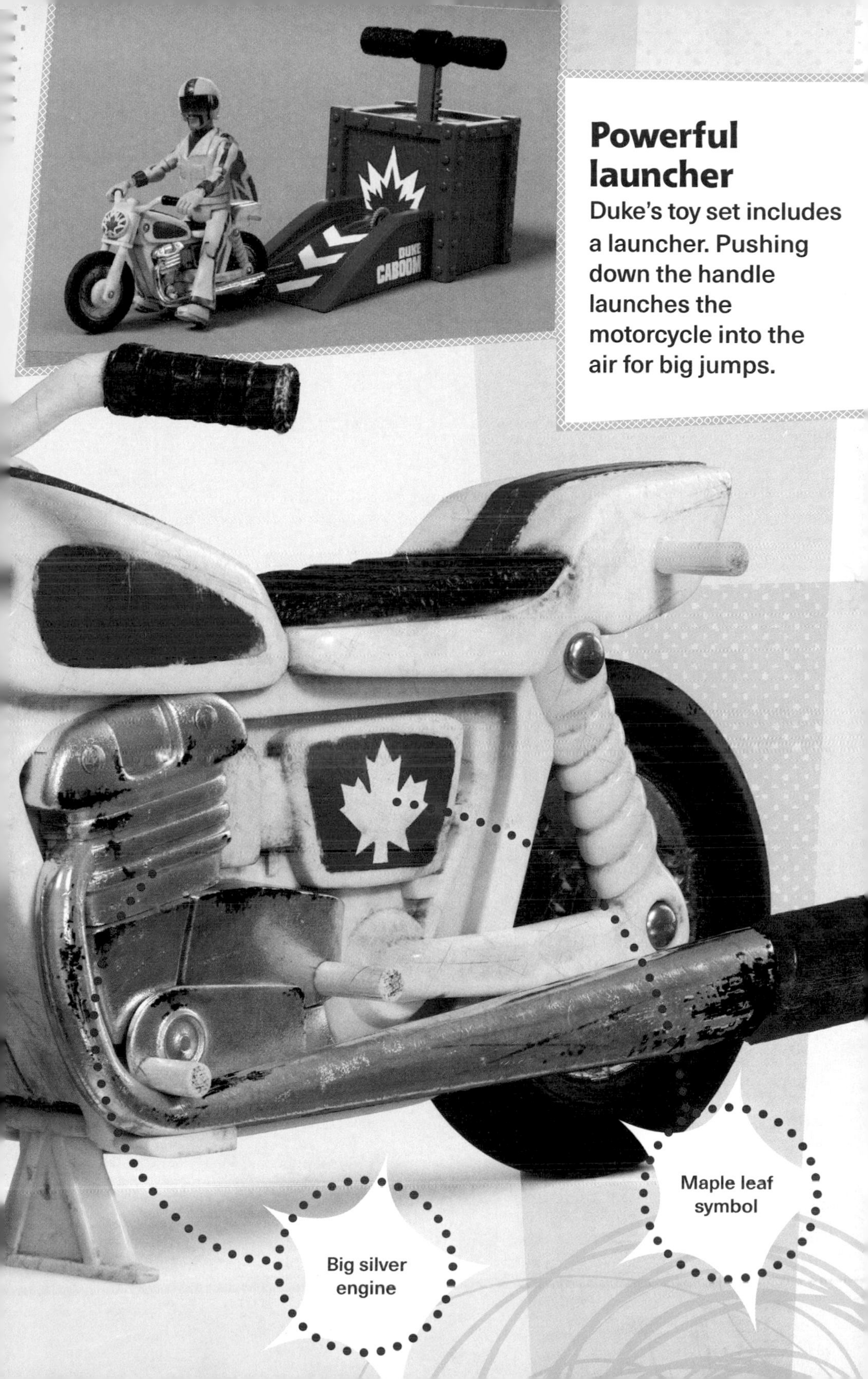

Powerful launcher

Duke's toy set includes a launcher. Pushing down the handle launches the motorcycle into the air for big jumps.

Daredevil poses

Duke Caboom loves to put on a show with his mighty motorcycle moves. He's Canada's greatest stuntman!

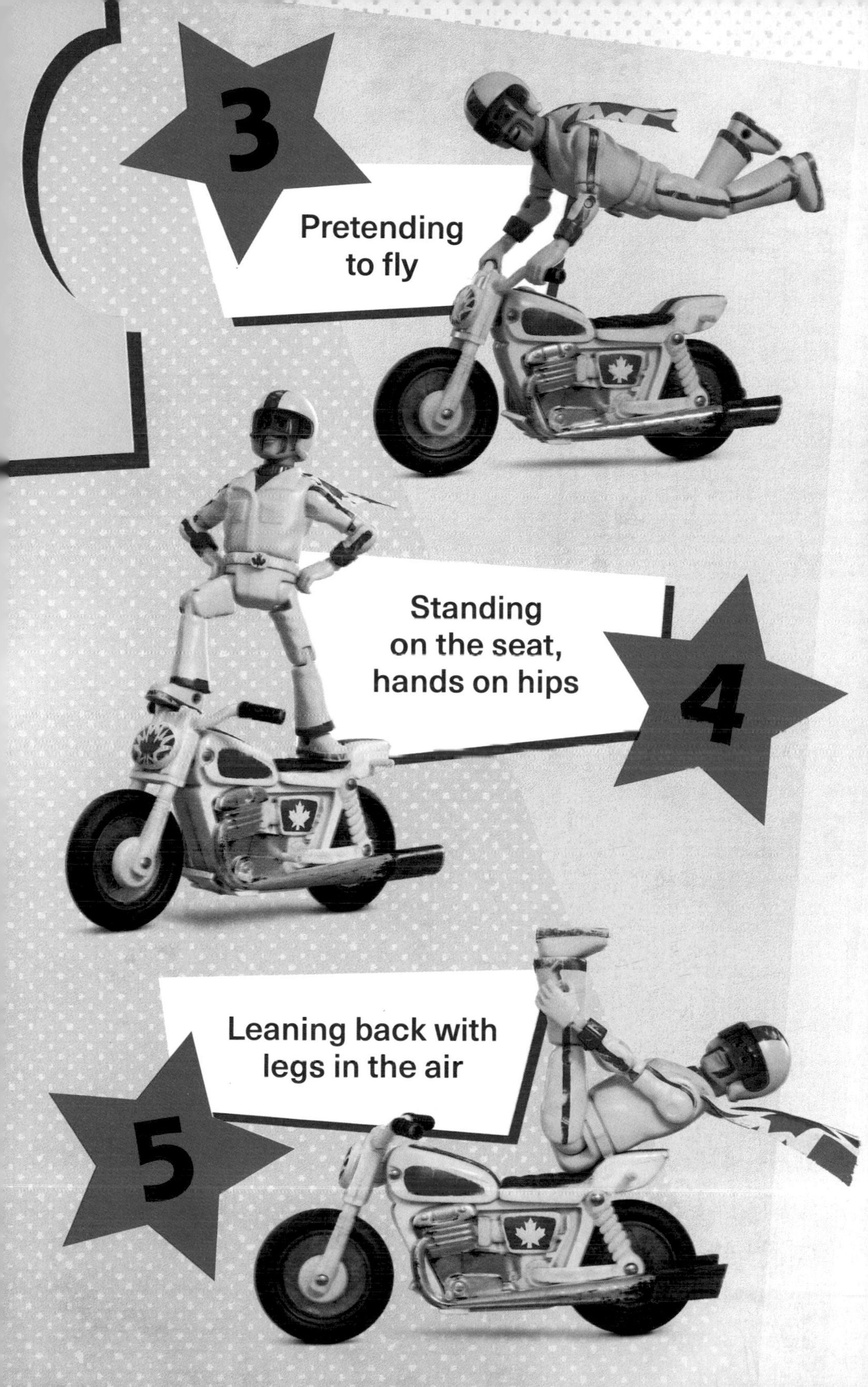
3
Pretending
to fly
Standing
on the seat,
hands on hips
4
Leaning back with
legs in the air
5

"What do we DO?!"

Mrs. Potato Head

Jessie

Quick-thinking cowgirl

Cheerful Jessie is supersmart. She is full of bright ideas to prevent Bonnie's family from leaving town before Woody has returned from his mission!

Things you need to know about Jessie

1 She greets Forky with her typical "Howdy!" when they first meet.

2 Jessie plays the part of the sheriff in Bonnie's town game.

3 She thinks of a great idea to make Bonnie's dad drive to the carnival, by getting Trixie to mimic the voice of the GPS. Turn right!

4 Jessie sneaks into Bonnie's backpack to keep an eye on her when she starts first grade.

Operation Flat Tire

Yikes! Bonnie's mom and dad are about to drive off—but Buzz and Woody are still not back from their mission to save Forky! What's a cowgirl to do?

1 Stay focused

Jessie focuses on the problem as the other toys argue and panic. She has a brilliant idea. Light bulb moment!

Bad ideas ...

Buttercup suggests the toys frame Dad for a crime so he gets put in jail. Rex suggests they go back in time to warn Woody about the future!

2 Travel to the target

Jessie jumps out of the RV's window and sneaks up to one of the front tires.

3 Identify target and attack

Jessie punctures the tire with a sharp nail. The air escapes, and the tire goes flat.

4 Return to safety

She returns to the back of the vehicle and climbs back through the window.

5 Enjoy the adoring crowd

The rest of the toys are amazed by her daring mission!

Living like Bo

Over the years, Bo has traveled far and wide, meeting different children and discovering new places. She has learned so much along the way!

DO live in the moment, and say yes to fun.
Piñata party? Why not?!

DO be prepared.
Bo collects repair supplies during her travels in case she gets broken during playtime.

DO make your own happiness.
Bo appreciates the small things in life, like a beautiful view.

DO be confident in your abilities.
Bo knows exactly which child will be a good match to play with a toy.

DO help others to see the best in themselves.
Bo encourages other toys to use their strengths.

DON'T rely on one kid to make you happy.
There are so many different kids out there with different interests.

DON'T waste time waiting for things to happen.
Bo and Giggle spent years on the shelf in the antiques store, waiting to be bought.

DON'T be afraid to try new things.
Bo travels from place to place and enjoys seeing new parts of the world.

DON'T always put others first, no matter the cost.
Bo knows it's important to look after herself as well as her friends.

Which toy are you?

Discover which awesome toy you are most like! Is it Duke Caboom, Bo Peep, or Woody?

1

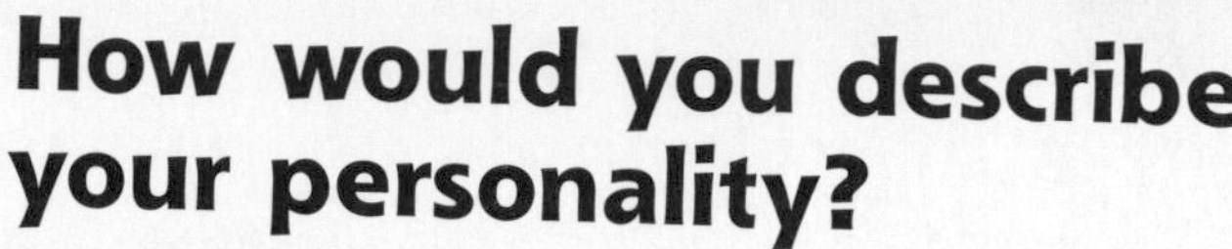

How would you describe your personality?

A A show-off

B Adventurous

C Loyal

2

You must take a risk to help a friend, but it's scary. Do you?

A Try to avoid the situation—but if you can't, then just hope for the best.

B Take your time—check out the situation, use your experience, and be confident.

C Go for it—your friend needs you right now, and there's no time to lose.

3

Pick an accessory!

A A helmet

B A cape

C A cowboy hat

What are your favorite hobbies?

A Acting and singing
B Exploring and building things
C Playing and being with friends

What do you find trickiest?

A Believing in yourself
B Admitting when you feel hurt
C Listening to others when you disagree with them

Mostly As—Duke Caboom

You love to be the star of the show and make people laugh. You're brave, but you don't always believe in yourself.

Mostly Bs—Bo Peep

You're a real adventurer and love trying new things. You're smart and know how to bring out the best in people.

Mostly Cs—Woody

You're super kind and would do anything for your friends. You never give up and always try your hardest.

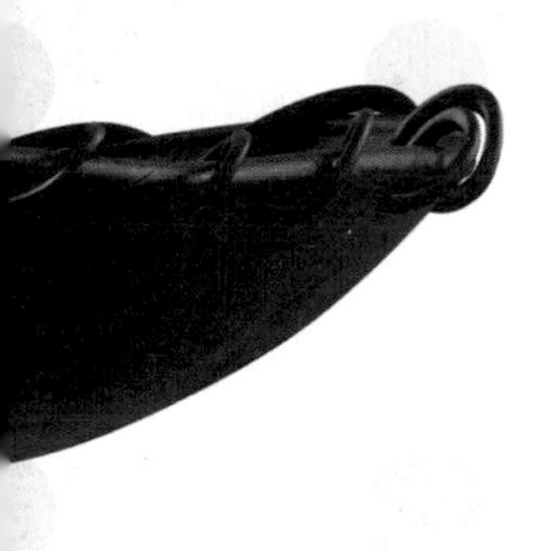

"You have this way of making a toy see the best in themselves."
Woody

Senior Editor Ruth Amos
Senior Designer Lynne Moulding
US Editor Jennette ElNaggar
Preproduction Producer Siu Yin Chan
Senior Producer Jonathan Wakeham
Managing Editor Sadie Smith
Managing Art Editor Vicky Short
Publisher Julie Ferris
Art Director Lisa Lanzarini
Publishing Director Simon Beecroft

First American Edition, 2019
Published in the United States by DK Publishing
1450 Broadway, Suite 801, New York, NY 10018

19 20 21 22 23 10 9 8 7 6 5 4 3 2 1
001–311502–May/2019

Published in Great Britain by Dorling Kindersley Limited.

A catalog record for this book is available from the Library of Congress.
ISBN 978-1-4654-7891-7

Printed and bound in the USA

A WORLD OF IDEAS:
SEE ALL THERE IS TO KNOW

www.dk.com
www.disney.com

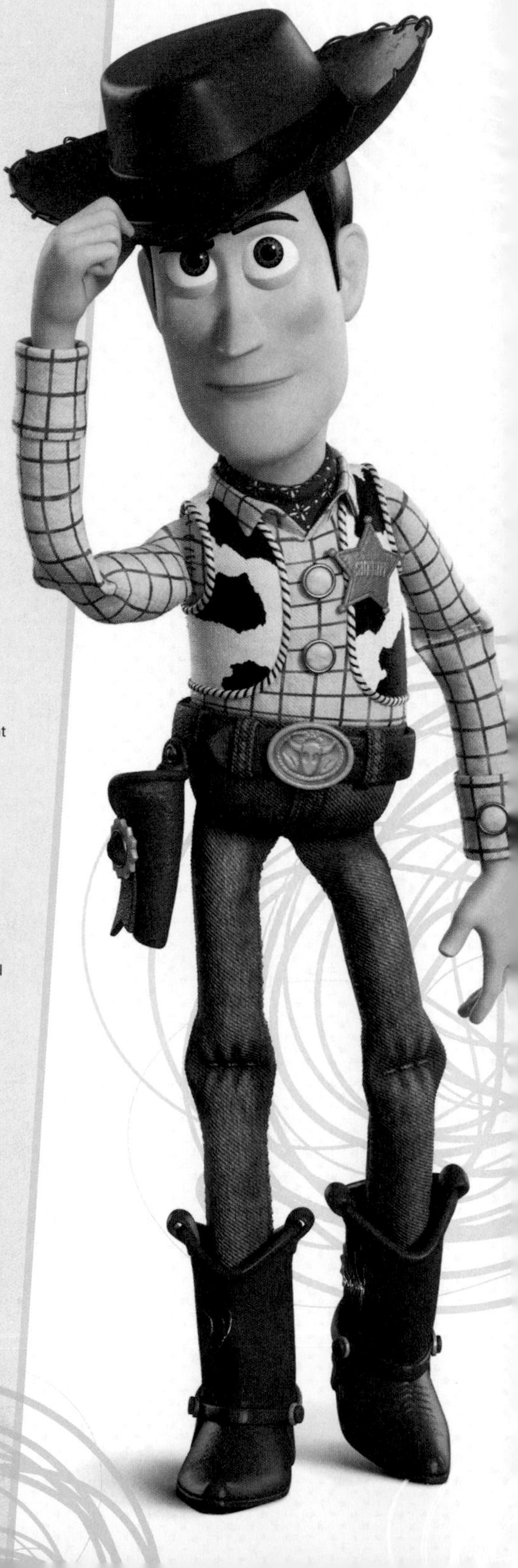